THE
KING'S
BISCUITS

BY
STEVE
PRIEST

The King's Biscuits
By Steve Priest

Illustrations by the author

Published by Steve Priest

First Published 2020 by Steve Priest

ISBN: 978-1-8381792-0-5

For Josh

Once upon a time there was a king,
and biscuits were his favourite thing.

He ate them morning, noon and night,
he had a greedy appetite.

But then one day the queen walked in,
"No biscuits in the biscuit tin!"

She told the king whose sad face frowned,
he called the Knights of Table Round.

They met around
the old tree stump,
they really were
an oddly clump.

He sent them
on a special mission,
a biscuit finding
expedition!

They searched the land and most did fail,

to find the king his holy grail.

But best of all the knights were three,
a finer bunch you'll never see.

They heard about
a dragon's treasure,
with lots of biscuits
for it's pleasure.

The three took turns
to try their hand,
for fame and fortune
in the land.

The first to dare the dragon's den, was quiet as a mouse

SPLISH SPLASH!

I'm brrrrrrr... COLD!

In crept Sir Squeak, and sneak sneak sneak...

He searched about the house.

Giant Cheese! ...keep going

THE SECRET ENTRANCE

SOFT CHEESE

CHUTN

HARD

The dragon had the best of ears,
and heard a sneaky sound.

It gave the knight an awful fright,
back home he leapt and bound.

The next to face the dragon's might
was brave, she was a lion.

She liked to use the lance a lot,
and charged with strength of iron.

The dragon knew a thing or two,
about a lion's pride.

tee hee hee!

It danced out of the way
and smiled.

It's grin grew
great and wide.

BOUNCE...

LEAP!

The Lady of the Lance flew past,
she couldn't win this game.

So off she went, to bed she ran...
to go and hide her shame.

Raynard he was a sly old fox,
the last to quest the biscuit box.

He entered in the dragon's lair,
with sharp green eyes and bright red hair.

He sang a song of cunning rhyme,
with clever words in quick quick time.

The tune it was of counting sheep,
a song to send the beast to sleep.

The dragon though, it was no fool
and filled it's ears with mortar.

It grabbed the knight, then took to flight
and dropped him in the water!

The knights had failed in their big test,
although they gave their very best.

The dragon had his champions beat,
the king was mad and stomped his feet.

He grabbed his sword, a fairy blade
and set off to the dragon's glade.

His trusty wizard by his side,
to help him win and be his guide.

The king he shouted at the dragon,
"Put the biscuits on my wagon!"

He banged his sword upon his shield,
but still the beast it would not yield.

The dragon puffed a gust of flame,
and bent the sword to end the game.

"Your silliness
is quite absurd...
you have to say
the magic word."

"Abracadabra, Ali Kazam! I've tried all words a good king can."

The wizard whispered in his ear, a special word the king did hear.

"PLEASE!"
said the king,
so loud and clear.

A magic word
to bring good cheer!

"I'm sorry that
I was so rude,
I really was
a naughty dude."

cool!

yeahy!

The dragon smiled and took a bow,
"I hope good friends we can be now...

I'd like to ask you 'round for tea,
and share my biscuits here with me."

The king was happy and clapped his hands,
his joy was heard throughout the lands.

He had the words put on his banners...

"It always pays to have...

GOOD MANNERS!"

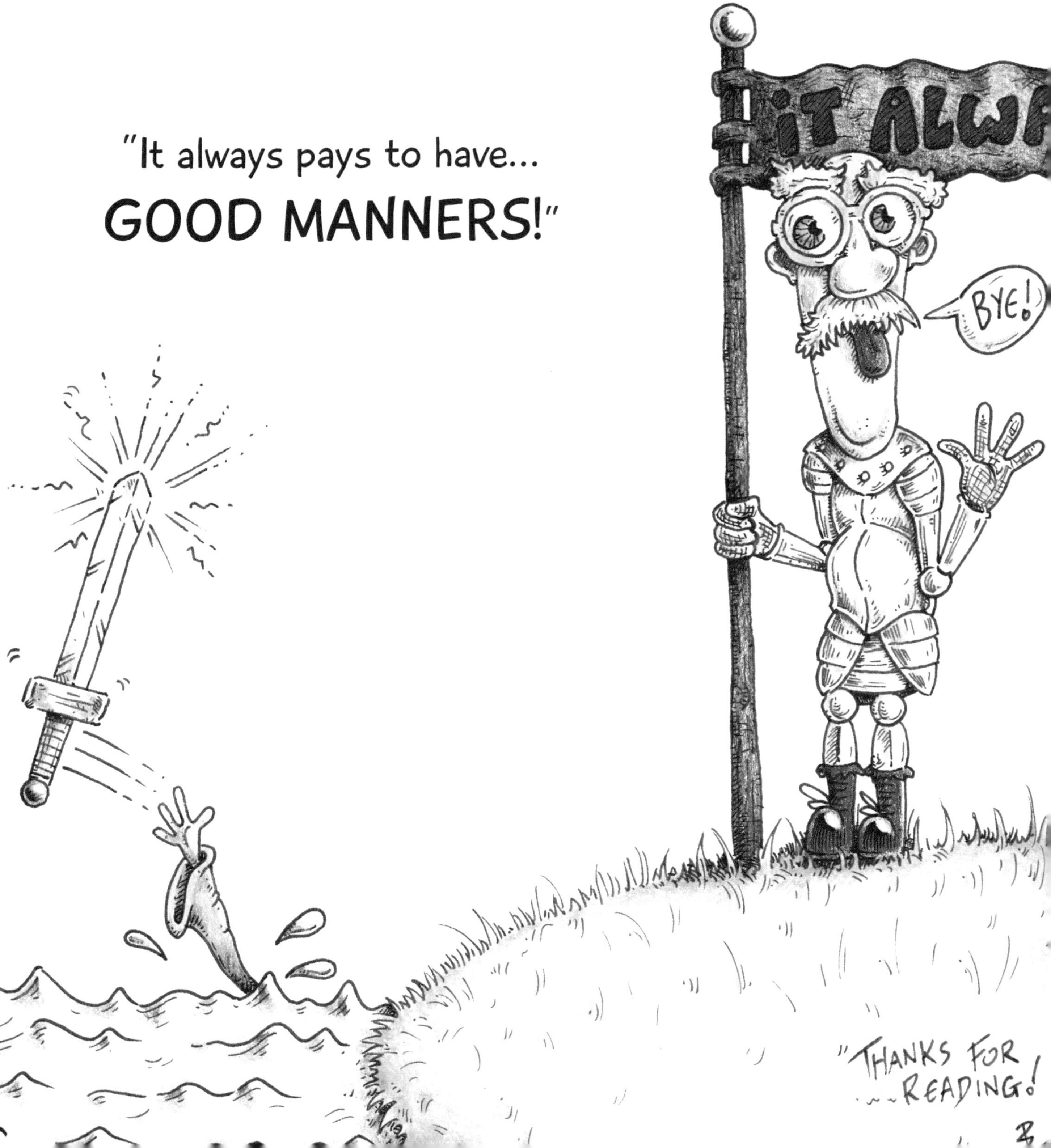

CPSIA information can be obtained
at www.ICGtesting.com
Printed in the USA
LVRC030326011220
672993LV00007BA/40